The Ghostly Bell Ringer

The Ghostly Bell Ringer

AND OTHER MYSTERIES
Compiled by the Editors
of
Highlights for Children

BOYDS MILLS PRESS

Compilation copyright © 1992 by Boyds Mills Press, Inc.
Contents copyright by Highlights for Children, Inc.
All rights reserved
Published by Boyds Mills Press, Inc.
A Highlights Company
910 Church Street
Honesdale, Pennsylvania 18431

Publisher Cataloging-in-Publication Data
Main entry under title.
The ghostly bell ringer : and other mysteries / compiled by the Editors of
Highlights for Children.
[96] p. : ill. ; cm.
Stories originally published in Highlights for Children.
Summary: A collection of mystery stories for young people.
ISBN 1-878093-39-8
[1. Detective and mystery stories] I. Highlights for Children. II. Title.
        [F]   1992
Library of Congress Catalog Card Number: 90-85915

Drawings by Judith Hunt
Distributed by St. Martin's Press
Printed in the United States of America

 2 3 4 5 6 7 8 9 10

Highlights® is a registered trademark of Highlights for Children, Inc.

CONTENTS

The Ghostly Bell Ringer

By Jeanette Brown

Ring! Ring!

Andy hurried to the front door. The steps were empty. "There's no one here," he called to his mother.

"Again? I'm getting tired of this," said Andy's mother, glancing outside. "That's about the tenth time in the past week that someone has rung the bell and disappeared."

"At least it's not so late this time," said Andy. "It's usually after ten at night." He closed the door.

"It's odd that Scamp didn't bark," said his mother. "He was right there in the yard. It must be one of your friends—someone we know."

"Nobody I know would do that!" said Andy indignantly.

"Then it has to be a ghost!" Andy's sister, Sarah, said. She laughed. "I did see something white last night, and of course Scamp couldn't smell a ghost."

That night Andy decided to catch the bell ringer. He needed a plan. His friend Bill lived right across the street. He could help watch. But it would take just as long to phone Bill when the doorbell rang as it would to get to the front door. It had to be something faster.

The tree house! If he slept there, he'd have a good view of the front door. And his mother let him sleep up there almost whenever he wanted to in the summer. Of course, it might be hard to see clearly in the dark. There should be some way of seeing who the bell ringer was.

The next morning Andy consulted his father. "Please, may I use your Polaroid camera with the flash? If I could just get a picture of our bell ringer, we'd have proof."

At first his father said no, but finally he

agreed. "Be careful. Don't break the camera or fall out of the tree house," he said.

Andy enlisted Sarah's help. "You stand by the front door and put your finger on the bell, and I'll focus on the right spot."

While Sarah posed, Andy got the camera all set. He anchored it firmly to the platform of the tree house. "Sarah, you'll have to signal me from inside with a flashlight when the bell rings. I can't hear it from up here."

That night Andy curled up on the platform. He lay awake for a long time, watching Sarah's window, but nothing happened. He kept worrying that Sarah would fall asleep but finally fell asleep himself. The next thing he knew, it was morning. The bell ringer must have skipped a night. He climbed down the ladder and found his mother in the kitchen.

"The bell didn't ring last night, did it?" he asked.

"Oh yes, it did! As usual, only later. About midnight. And Scamp never barked." She frowned. "I even looked around the yard for something ghostly. And I saw that glimpse of something white again."

Sarah appeared, rubbing her eyes, just in time to hear. She and Andy looked at each other. They didn't say anything, but they both wondered if it *could* be a ghost.

That night they tried Plan Number Two. Andy tied one end of a long cord to Sarah's finger and the other end to his own thumb. They would take turns jerking on the cord to keep each other awake.

Andy climbed into the tree house, fastened the camera securely again, and focused it on the front door. He settled down for a long wait, his thumb ready. But he'd barely taken his position when a bright streak of light flashed into his eyes. Sarah was using the flashlight—on, off, on, off. Andy snapped a picture quickly. The flash worked beautifully. He could see a dim figure on the porch but couldn't make out who it was. By the time he clambered down the tree, the bell ringer was gone.

Sarah came dashing out the door. Scamp was there, too, running back and forth. "Did you get it?" she asked anxiously.

"I think so." Eagerly they waited for the camera to develop its picture. Andy pulled it out with shaking fingers. "Look!"

"No!" They both stared at the snapshot. "It can't be!" But it was. There was Scamp, standing on his hind feet, poking at the bell with his front paw, his white coat gleaming in the light of the camera flash.

"No wonder he didn't bark," said Sarah. "He wouldn't bark at himself!"

Andy stood thinking a minute. "Well, I don't blame him. He doesn't like being kept outside. It was much nicer for Scamp when he was a puppy and stayed inside with us. He must have watched how visitors get into the house and copied them!"

Sarah agreed. "He's a smart dog!"

Andy rang the bell again and put his head in the doorway. "Mother, you were right! The bell ringer *is* someone we know!"

"Look, Mother," called Sarah. "Here's our ghost."

Riddle
of the
Missing Piece

By Kathleen Stevens

Miho twisted in her seat to steal a look at the classroom clock. Two minutes till the bell and then—the final round of the puzzle contest. Her glasses were slipping down her nose. She pushed them back in place without thinking. In her imagination Miho was seeing the blue water and colored sailboats of her team's jigsaw puzzle.

Suddenly the bell rang. "Are you ready?"

Diana asked as they moved toward the door.

"We're way behind," Lisa added. "If 5B finishes their puzzle first, we lose."

Miho smiled shyly, pleased that the girls had spoken to her. "I went to the library before school this morning to study the puzzle."

Lisa's brown eyes were approving. "Great idea!"

Mrs. Cole had thought so, too. The librarian was one of the few people Miho felt comfortable with in her new school. Only Mrs. Cole knew how hard it was for Miho to make friends.

This morning when Miho had walked into the library, past the custodian with her vacuum and dust rags, Mrs. Cole was at her desk. When Miho explained what she wanted, Mrs. Cole was delighted. "You're the first contestant who has thought of studying the puzzle ahead of time, Miho. Good strategy!"

Miho had gone over to the table where the two puzzles were spread out. The mountain scene that 5B was doing had many more pieces already together than 5A's harbor view. Miho studied her class's puzzle carefully, checking loose pieces against the picture on the box and looking for shapes to fill empty spots. She wanted so badly to do well in this contest.

Now Lisa reminded her. "We need these points, Miho. If you win, our class will be the champions of Challenge Week."

"Good luck!" added Diana.

As they started toward the library, students spilled out of the doorway of 5B. Miho heard a red-headed boy say, "We're bound to win! We're ahead, and Anita's fast." Suddenly Miho felt nervous. Could she really catch up?

In the library a pretty girl with curly hair was standing behind the puzzle table. That must be Anita, Miho thought.

Mrs. Cole raised her hand for silence. "Today we finish the final event in Fifth-Grade Challenge Week. Every day this week two different players have worked on the puzzles. The player who finishes first today will win the event for her class."

The red-headed boy called out, "Okay, Anita, do your stuff!" A burst of cheers came from 5B.

Then Miho heard Diana's voice. "Anita may be good, but so is Miho. She even came in this morning to study the puzzle. If anyone can win for us, she can!"

Lisa leaned forward. "Come on, Miho!"

Miho flushed with pleasure as her classmates called encouragement. She would do her best.

Mrs. Cole held up a stopwatch. "Ready . . . go!"

First the yellow piece. That was part of the sun. Then the red piece. It belonged to the sailboat. Swiftly Miho reached for pieces she had studied and pressed them into place. Her hands flew over the puzzle. Maybe she could win. Maybe she really could.

Suddenly Anita called, "Time out!"

Miho looked up in surprise.

"What's the problem?" Mrs. Cole asked.

Anita pointed to her puzzle. "I need a green piece for the bush. Nothing left is the right color."

"Are you sure?" Mrs. Cole studied Anita's puzzle. Then she checked the floor underneath the table. "You're right. That piece isn't here."

"Maybe it was missing all along," Miho suggested.

Frowning, Mrs. Cole shook her head. "I did both these puzzles on Monday. No pieces were missing."

There was a long silence. Then Anita turned to Miho. "Didn't Diana say you came in to study the puzzle this morning?"

A murmur ran through the crowd of boys and girls, and someone muttered, "Maybe Miho took the piece so she'd be sure to win."

A lump filled Miho's throat as she looked at the ring of staring faces.

Mrs. Cole touched her shoulder. "Miho, I don't believe you took that puzzle piece. But what could have happened to it?"

Her eyes smarting with tears, Miho shook her head. How could anyone know where the missing piece had gone? Miho remembered Mrs. Cole's pleased smile when she told Miho how wise it was to study the puzzle. And suddenly Miho remembered something else. "The custodian! She was carrying out the vacuum when I came in here this morning," Miho said. "Maybe the puzzle piece fell on the floor and the vacuum sucked it up."

Mrs. Cole thought for a moment. "Martin," she said to the red-haired boy from 5B. "Go down to the boiler room. Ask Miss Garrity to check the vacuum cleaner bag."

To Miho it seemed like hours until Martin reappeared. He stood in the doorway, his face solemn. Then he grinned and held up his hand. "Here's the missing piece!"

A cheer went up from Miho's classmates.

Mrs. Cole turned to the two girls. "Shall we get back to business? Ready . . ."

Miho looked at her grinning classmates and reached for a puzzle piece. No matter how the contest turned out, she already felt like a winner.

The Secret Hiding Place

By June Swanson

Carrying his shoes, Jeff tiptoed along the dark hall. He was almost afraid to breathe. If he woke Grandma and Grandpa, they would never let him go outside alone—not at four o'clock in the morning. When he reached the stairs, he felt for the first step with his foot. He had to get downstairs and outside without waking them. He had to find that secret hiding place.

Jeff had spent the whole week looking. He had searched the whole house—even the basement and the attic and the garage. And now Mom would be here in a few hours to pick him up. This was his last chance.

"Jeff, I need your help," Grandpa had said last week when Jeff first came to spend his vacation with his grandparents. "Seems the man who used to own this house had a large collection of rare coins. But when he died and his son came to clean out the house, the son couldn't find it. His father had once written that the collection was hidden in a secret place in the house."

"A secret hiding place? Here?" Jeff had cried.

Grandpa nodded and continued. "Shortly after that, the son was killed in an accident. He had no heirs, and no one else ever looked for the collection. Now we own the house . . . and the collection, too. If we ever find it, that is."

"Wow!" was all Jeff could say.

"But I painted everything from the ceiling to the floor when we moved in," Grandpa said. "I covered every inch of this house, and I didn't find any secret hiding place."

"Did you check the bookcases?" Jeff asked. "In mystery stories, bookcases always have secret panels or something."

Grandpa smiled. "Sorry. There isn't a bookcase in the house."

"Don't worry. I'll find that hiding place for you," Jeff promised.

"I hope so," Grandpa had said. "I'm counting on you."

That had made Jeff feel important.

But now he would be leaving in a few hours, and he hadn't found the hiding place.

Jeff had hardly slept all night. Then, just a few minutes ago, he had suddenly had an idea. That old cabinet in the garage! He hadn't looked at it closely. It was the perfect place for a secret compartment.

The first step squeaked slightly as he stepped on it. Jeff stopped, but there was no sound from Grandma and Grandpa's room. The next step squeaked, too, but it wasn't as noisy as the first one. Finally, he was almost down. As he put his foot on the last step, it sagged and creaked loudly. Jeff jumped. And then froze. He could feel his heart pounding. But again no sound came from upstairs.

As quietly as he could, Jeff unlocked the front door and slipped out, being careful to leave it unlocked so he could get back in. He put on his shoes and took his flashlight from the pocket of his bathrobe.

Soon Jeff was in the garage. He flashed his light over the cabinet. It looked mysterious in the dark. That collection just had to be here. Jeff tapped along one side, listening for a hollow sound. He tapped across the top, down the other side, and then along the bottom. Everything sounded solid. He went over it again. He checked all the shelves. Nothing.

Disappointed, Jeff stepped back and stared at the cabinet. It had been his last hope. Grandpa was counting on him to help, and he hadn't done it.

Slowly Jeff walked back to the house. Once inside, he took off his shoes and started up the stairs. *Creak!* He had forgotten that bottom step. Jeff ran up the rest of the stairs as fast as he could and jumped into bed. Muffled voices came from the next room. Grandma and Grandpa were awake! Had they already looked in his room?

He heard footsteps outside his door and Grandpa clearing his throat. Jeff closed his eyes, pretending to be asleep. From the squeaking sounds, he knew Grandpa was going downstairs. *Creak!* went that bottom step.

Why would anybody build such a creaky old step, anyway? Jeff wondered. Suddenly Jeff sat straight up in bed. Of course! It was in one of his mystery books. A secret step! In one leap Jeff was out of bed and running. "Grandpa," he yelled, "I bet the secret hiding place is in the bottom step!"

Grandpa stood at the foot of the stairs with a glass of milk in his hand and a surprised look on his face.

"See?" Jeff asked excitedly, stamping on the bottom step. "Doesn't it sound different from the rest?"

"You're right!" Now Grandpa was excited, too. He stooped and ran his fingers around the step. "This top board is loose."

"I bet it slides out," Jeff said, "just like in my book." He pulled the board toward him, and it slowly came out. "Grandpa, look!" Jeff held up a gold coin.

Super Sleuth Samantha

By Jennifer Schulze

Sam hung the carefully lettered sign on the door of her playhouse. She picked up her paintbrush and put the lid back on her jar of green paint. She sat down at her desk, put on her most serious sleuthing expression, and picked up a pencil. She rested her elbow on the edge of the desk and waited for her first case.

Sam waited for a long time. But no clients knocked at her door. She stood up and paced quietly. The time passed slowly. And still no one came. Sam was beginning to get hungry. It was close to lunchtime by now. And she hadn't had one single case to solve.

Then, just as she was about to give up, there came a soft tapping at the door. Sam held her breath and waited. Yes, there it was again. Someone was knocking on the door!

Her first case? Sam rushed to the door and flung it open. But there was no one there at all. Frowning, Sam peered around the doorway. She looked to the right and to the left. There was no one in sight. Disappointed, Sam was about to close the door again when she glanced down. There on the doorstep was a small brown shoe box.

"Aha," said Sam cheerfully, "this seems to be a mystery."

Cautiously, Sam lifted the box and set it on the desk. Then just as carefully, she opened the mysterious box. There were three small objects in it. This is puzzling, thought Sam as she took them out one by one. First she pulled out a locket on a thin gold chain. Sam picked up her magnifying glass and examined it carefully. It seemed to be an ordinary locket. No clues there. The second object was a juicy yellow lemon, and the third was a small piece of lace.

That's odd, thought Sam. There doesn't appear to be any connection between these clues. But she opened her pad and wrote down what she had found. *Clue number one,* wrote Sam, *locket, lemon, lace.* Well, they all begin with the same letter, Sam thought. Perhaps that's a connection.

There was something scribbled in the bottom of the empty shoe box. A message! The message said *Look for your next clue under the maple tree.* Sam returned all of the items to the shoe box. Then she put the pencil, pad, and magnifying glass into her pocket. Sam was ready to solve her first case.

In the front yard under the maple tree, Sam found a tiny glass unicorn, an umbrella, and a map of the United States. The note here instructed her to go to the sandbox. Sam wrote the clues down neatly: *unicorn, umbrella, United States.*

Sam placed the map and the unicorn in her clue box. She hung the umbrella over her arm.

At the sandbox Sam found a paper napkin, a nut, a shiny new nickel, and a note telling her to look in the mailbox.

Inside the mailbox she discovered a red crayon, a comb, and a toy car. Each time she found that the three clues began with the same letter. Sam wrote down all the clues she had uncovered.

The last clues were on the porch steps, where Sam discovered an old hat, a horseshoe, and a hammer. She sat down on the bottom step and rested her chin in her hands. This was a tough case, and Sam was getting awfully hungry. But she wasn't going to give up. A good detective never quits a case, Sam told herself.

Trying to shut out the tempting smell of hamburgers cooking in the kitchen, Sam took the note pad out of her pocket. She studied the clues she had written down:

Clue number one: locket, lemon, lace
Clue number two: unicorn, umbrella, United States
Clue number three: napkin, nut, nickel
Clue number four: crayon, comb, car
Clue number five: hat, horseshoe, hammer

Sam thought very hard. She thought and thought and thought. Her stomach growled again. Suddenly, Sam sat up very straight. Her notebook closed with a snap. She had solved the case.

Sam put the clues into the box. She hooked the umbrella over her arm and opened the kitchen door. Dad was just setting two plates on the table, and he smiled when Sam walked in.

"Now then, Super Sleuth Samantha," said Dad, "what are you ready for?"

"L-U-N-C-H," said Sam.

The Mystery of the Lost Voice

By Pauline Watson

One lazy Saturday afternoon, Richard sat on his unmade bed and admired a smooth brown rock that had just come in the mail.

He was still holding the rock in the palm of his hand when Angelo, who lived next door, bounced into the bedroom without knocking. "Richard, do you want to play ball? Hey, what's that?" he asked, pointing to the rock. "A new pet?"

Richard grinned. "Better than that," he said dreamily. "This rock is magic. It grants wishes."

"Oh sure!" Angelo snorted. "That's fairy-tale stuff . . ."

"Wrong!" Richard cut in. "This rock really *is* magic!"

"So are dragons," said Angelo dryly. "Listen!" His voice rose suddenly. "The guys are meeting at the park for a ball game. Do you want to catch?"

Richard hopped off the bed. "As soon as I wish on my rock," he said. He tapped the rock with his index finger and added, "Let me see . . . what should I wish for?"

"Brains," offered Angelo.

"Quiet!" snapped Richard. "I'm thinking."

"How can you believe that stuff?" Angelo asked.

"The magazine ad said so. This rock is guaranteed," Richard said. His face brightened. "I have a wish," he said.

"Rub it carefully," Angelo said and laughed.

"I wish you'd be quiet!" Richard yelled. He stopped rubbing the rock, pursed his lips, and glared at Angelo. The grin left Angelo's face. His eyes blinked.

"What's wrong with you?" Richard asked when

Angelo's mouth flew open. But Angelo didn't answer.

Richard slipped the rock into a pocket of his jeans. "No sense in trying to work magic with a clown around," he said, feeling disgusted. "Come on, quit acting silly, and let's go." Angelo pointed to his mouth and shook his head.

Richard's eyes narrowed. "Are you trying to tell me that you can't talk?"

Angelo nodded. The puzzled look left Richard's face. He laughed. "This rock really *is* magic!" he shouted.

He pulled it from his pocket, placed it in the palm of his left hand, and said, "No problem. I'll have you talking again in a snap." With the flair of a magician he waved his right hand, brought it down upon the rock, and fluttered his fingers over it. Then he began to rub the rock slowly. "Oh, rock," he said, "I wish Angelo had his voice back."

Chuckling, Richard pushed the bedspread over and sat down on his bed, still holding the rock. Then he looked up at Angelo. "Let's go," he said. Angelo's feet looked as if they were glued to the carpet, but his lips started to move. First they widened, then they puckered, and then they gaped.

"Stop the fish faces!" cried Richard. Angelo's eyes bulged. His lips moved again, but no sound

33

came from his throat. Richard looked startled. "You really can't talk!" he whispered. "This is awful! What'll I do?" Angelo sat in the white cane-backed chair and folded his hands.

"I'll read the directions again," Richard said. He removed a small card from the rock box. He read, "'Here is the Super Magnetic Wishing Rock that you ordered. Simply rub and make a wish. Guaranteed.'" On the bottom of the card was the address of the company, KCOR, Inc.

Richard grabbed the rock, rubbed it, and wished again. Nothing happened. Downstairs the telephone rang, and soon his mother's voice called, "Richard, Angelo is wanted on the phone!" Richard went to the den and answered the phone.

It was Jake wanting to play ball. "We're coming soon," Richard promised.

He went back to his room and begged, "Angelo, please say something. Anything! Can you grunt?" Angelo moved his lips. They widened, then puckered, then gaped. Next came the fish faces. Following that came something that looked to Richard like monkey faces.

Richard swallowed a grin. "I have magic to fix your voice," he said, and he disappeared into his closet. In a few seconds he came growling into the room wearing a Halloween monster mask and waving his arms wildly. There was fresh command in his voice when he ordered, "Speak!"

Angelo looked at him and shook his head. That made Richard growl louder. Like a monster gone wild, he grabbed the spread and threw it over his friend's head. "Captured!" Richard snarled, and he fell to his knees. He began to tickle the squirming lump.

"Quit! Stop it!" Angelo yelled as he struggled to free himself from the spread. "Have you gone bananas?"

Richard took the spread off Angelo's face. "Maybe it was foolish to buy the rock," he said, grinning. "But at least I'm not *completely* stupid!"

"I'm glad," said Angelo. "So come on. Get your glove and let's play ball!"

The Mail-Slot Mystery

By Jeffie Ross Gordon

Shannon sat at the dining room table. It seemed to take so long to do homework. She chewed on the end of her pencil. "How much is eight times eight?" she muttered. "I can never remember." Suddenly she heard a noise. It came from the front porch. Then she heard the mail slot creak.

Shannon went to the door. Before she opened it, she saw a pink slip of paper poking from the mail slot. She pulled it out and unfolded it.

PLEA SECO METO MYB IRTH DAYP ART
YONS ATURDA YAT ONEKA TIER OBINS ON
WE AR AD ISGUISE IT ISA MY STE RYP ART Y.
EEE-GBCH.

Shannon scratched her head. "PLEA SECO?
What does that mean?" She opened the front
door and looked out. There was no one there.

"Shannon, is your homework finished?" called
her mother.

"No," Shannon answered, "but almost."

Back at the table she turned the pink paper
over to use for scrap paper for her arithmetic
figuring. On the back, in large black letters, were
the words   SHANNON McGUIRE, IMPORTANT,
ANSWER BY THURSDAY. "Answer? Answer
what?" Shannon looked at the paper again. Was
this a language she didn't know? Maybe it was
Spanish. "I'll ask Pedro. He speaks Spanish.
Maybe he can read this," said Shannon.

Shannon hurried to finish her homework. "I'm
finished, Mom," she called. "I'm going to Pedro's
house."

"Be home in time for dinner," answered her
mother.

Shannon ran all the way. Pedro was practicing
the piano. Shannon had to wait for him to finish.

"Done." Pedro closed the cover over the keys.
From the top of the piano he took a piece of

blue paper. "Hey, Shannon," he said, "look at this."

Shannon held out the pink paper. She and Pedro compared the notes. Except for the names on the back, both papers said the same thing. "I thought maybe this was written in Spanish," Shannon said.

"No," said Pedro. "I think it might be Japanese."

"Kiku," they both said together. "She'll know."

Pedro and Shannon hurried to Kiku's house. She was in the front yard jumping rope. "Hey, Kiku," called Pedro, "we need your help."

"You made me lose count," she said, letting the rope go limp.

"Sorry," said Shannon. "We were wondering— can you read Japanese?"

"A little bit. And my mother can. What are you trying to read?"

Shannon and Pedro took the colored papers from their pockets. "These," they said.

"I have one, too," said Kiku, "and this isn't anything like Japanese. Japanese writing doesn't even look like this."

"How does it look?" asked Shannon.

Kiku went inside and brought out a Japanese book. Shannon and Pedro looked. "You're right," said Pedro. "Our notes are not Japanese."

"Then what are they?" asked Shannon.

"I think they're in code," said Kiku.

"A secret code?" asked Pedro.

"Real secret. We can't read it," said Shannon.

"Maybe Anthony can read it," said Kiku. "He reads a lot of mystery stories." She put the Japanese book back in the house. When she returned, she said, "I called. Anthony is home, and he has one of these, too."

"Let's go," said Shannon.

At Anthony's house they sat around the kitchen table. Together they read the words aloud.

"The next-to-last line! Start with IT ISA," said Kiku excitedly.

The four chanted the words aloud.

"It is a mystery party!" shouted Pedro.

"The words are all run together, then separated wrong," said Shannon. "See if we can figure out the rest."

"Please come . . .," began Anthony slowly.

". . . to myb? . . . to my birthday party . . .," continued Pedro.

"Saturday—on Saturday at one. Katie Robinson," read Kiku.

"Wear a disguise," they finished together.

"Terrific!" said Kiku.

"But what is EEE-GBCH?" asked Shannon. "Here at the bottom?"

"That's definitely code," said Anthony. "What's missing from this invitation?"

"An address?" asked Pedro.

"We all know where Katie lives," said Kiku.

"A phone number," said Shannon.

"E is the fifth letter in the alphabet. Our exchange is 555," said Pedro. "What about GBCH?"

Anthony took a paper and pencil. Quickly he wrote

1 2 3 4 5 6 7 8 9 0

A B C D E F G H I J

"It's 555-7238," he announced.

"That's it! Katie's phone number," said Kiku.

"Let's call," said Pedro.

"No," said Shannon, "let's answer her the same way. Do you have more paper, Anthony?"

"Yes."

They all helped write the answer.

"This sounds good," said Shannon when they had finished. She read it: "WEW ILL BEG LAD TOCO METO YO URP ART YONS ATURD AY. 1-14-20-8-15-14-25, 11-9-11-21, 19-8-1-14-14-15-14, 16-5-4-18-15. Should we put this in Katie's mail slot?"

"Yes. Let's go!" shouted the others in unison.

The Key in the Heart Mystery

By Marilyn Kratz

"Hey, Mom! Look at the big box the delivery person left!" shouted Greg.

"It's from your uncle Paul," said Mom as she removed an envelope from the top of the box.

"I'll get the scissors to open the box," said Greg. When he returned, his mother was reading the letter.

"Uncle Paul finally sold your grandparents' farm," said Mom. "He has sent me some things he found in the attic of the farmhouse. He says there's a treasure in this box for you, too, Greg."

"Wow!" exclaimed Greg as he cut the tape binding the box. "Does he say anything about that trip he promised me to his ranch in Wyoming?"

"Not one word about that," replied Mom.

Greg opened the box. He started unpacking it, keeping his eyes open for his treasure.

"Here's my mother's wedding gown, and these were some of my baby clothes," Mom said. "And here's my old scrapbook!"

Mom sat on the floor and began to look at the scrapbook while Greg unpacked some old books and photographs. "What's this?" Greg asked, lifting a small wooden dresser from the box.

"My mother's toy dresser!" said Mom. "Her father made it from the center of a huge walnut tree after it was broken in half by a tornado."

"Here's my treasure!" exclaimed Greg. He took a small metal chest from the box. Taped to the top was a note.

To Greg
A treasure awaits you in this box,
But a key to the lock is a must.
You have until the end of this month.
Look in a heart left by a gust.

Greg read the mysterious note aloud. "What does it mean?" he asked.

"I don't know," said Mom with a quiet smile. "But it's just like that brother of mine to add a touch of mystery. He often pretended he was a detective when we were kids."

Greg shook the metal chest, but not a sound came from within it. He pushed and pulled at the latch, but it would not move. Greg read the note again. "The end of this month—that's only three days away!" Greg said. "I'll have to find the clues in this note soon!"

Greg thought about the note as he helped his mother carry the contents of the box into the den. "The clues I need to find that key must be in the last line of the riddle," Greg decided. "It says I must look in a heart left by a gust. Was there anything heart-shaped in the box?"

"I don't think so," said Mom. "But I'll leave all these things here for the next three days so you can examine them."

Greg began to spend every spare minute in the den. He invited several of his friends to help him work on the clues. But no matter how hard they searched, they could not find the key.

After supper on the last day of the month, Greg returned to the den and read the note for what seemed like the hundredth time. "Look in a heart left by a gust," he read. "What clue is hidden in those simple words?" Greg decided to look up the words *heart* and *gust* in a dictionary, even though he was sure he knew what they meant.

The definitions for the word *heart* filled an entire column. Greg read it carefully. At the end was a list of synonyms for the word. One of them caught his attention. "Center," he read. "That's it! The key isn't in anything heart-shaped. It's in the *center* of something."

Next Greg found the word *gust*. "Sudden, strong rush of wind," he read. Then he remembered what Mom had said about the toy dresser that had belonged to her mother. It had been made from the center—the *heart*—of a tree broken in a tornado. And a tornado was a strong *gust* of wind.

Greg's fingers trembled with excitement as he picked up the little dresser. He had looked through it many times in the last three days. But this time he examined it inch by inch. He tilted the little mirror on the top. Nothing there. He ran his fingers along the pink felt lining in each drawer. No suspicious lumps. He shook it gently. No rattles. Greg removed the drawers and looked inside the dresser. "Whoopee! Here it is!" he shouted as he spied a small silver key taped to the inside of the dresser.

Quickly, he unlocked the metal chest. The lid

snapped up. The box was empty—except for a narrow envelope taped to the bottom. Greg opened the envelope. Out fell an airline ticket.

"Mom, Dad! Look!" Greg shouted, running to the living room. "A ticket to fly to Laramie, Wyoming. Uncle Paul wants me to visit him on his ranch!"

Dad examined the ticket. "Sure enough," he said. "And it's for next week."

Greg laughed as he said, "I got to the *heart* of that mystery just in time."

The Secret of the Summer Clock

By Linda Stankard-Green

The old lake house we were renting for the summer had a neglected, mysterious look. The hedges and lawn were so overgrown they seemed to be trying to hide the house from the outside world.

I felt like an intruder as the five of us clambered up the rickety porch steps with our suitcases. Dad struggled with the lock, but the door finally creaked open. Lara, the youngest, was afraid to go in, so David and I went first. Inside it was dark and damp, and there was a funny smell like old, wet newspapers.

"Hey, Lara!" I said, running back out to the porch. "Come on in. There's a loft inside!"

Lara walked hesitantly into the living room, where Mom was already busy pushing back drapes and opening windows. The sunlight brightened the place, and it didn't look so gloomy. Suddenly we heard a thunderous noise. The floorboards rumbled under our feet, and the dishes clinked in the cupboards.

"It's an earthquake!" Lara shrieked.

"Calm down," Dad said. "We passed the station on the way in. It's just a train going by."

"Let's go up to the loft, Lara," I said. We climbed the ladder and looked down at the living room.

"Hey, Dave," I said, calling over the railing. "Is it okay if Lara and I take this room?"

"Sure, Meg," he said, tilting his head back to look at us. "I'll take this one below you."

Just then I noticed the clock. It was an old wooden one with Roman numerals, and it was directly across from us, hung high on the wall on the other side of the living room. Lara noticed it too.

"Why is the little glass door to the clock

open?" she asked.

"I don't know," I said. "But chime clocks have to be wound, so maybe the last person to wind it forgot to close it."

"Maybe a ghost flew up and opened it," Lara whispered.

"I doubt it," I said, trying to keep my voice at a normal level. "But whoever opened it probably needed a ladder to reach it way up there."

"That's right, Meg," David said as he unhooked the ladder from our loft and placed it against the opposite wall.

"Now we're stranded up here!" Lara cried, clutching my arm.

"Take it easy, Lara. I'll put the ladder back in a minute." David climbed up and peered inside the clock. "Here's the key," he said, holding it out for us to see.

"My watch says 12:15," I called over to him. "You should set it to the right time." The clock had stopped at 12:05.

David set it at the correct time and wound it with the key. "Maybe it stopped just as we came into the house," he said. "Maybe there *are* ghosts here."

"Don't be silly, David. Besides, you're scaring Lara."

"Well," he said, giving the pendulum a little push, "let's see if it works." The little gold disk began to swing back and forth with a slow, steady rhythm.

"Hurray!" Lara cried, clapping her hands.

"We learned about pendulums last year," David said, replacing the ladder. "They have to be level to work."

"It's a beautiful old clock," I said, following Lara down to the living room.

We unloaded the car and there was a lot of

unpacking to do; it took us all day to get settled in. The last thing I remembered hearing was the ten deep bongs of the clock before I drifted off to sleep.

The next day we went to the lake. Dad took David and me out in the rowboat, while Mom and Lara stayed on the beach. It was late afternoon by the time the five of us started on our way back to the house.

"Well, I'll be a . . . Meg, come here," David said, pulling me aside and pointing to the clock. A knot formed in my stomach. The glass door was open again, and the clock had stopped at exactly 12:05.

"Don't say anything to Lara," I said, lowering my voice. "She already thinks the house is haunted."

"I'm beginning to wonder myself," said David.

When no one was looking, he took the ladder from the loft and reset the clock once again. The pendulum swung back and forth with a measured precision. "This is really peculiar. It was working fine this morning, so it couldn't have stopped at midnight. Let's come back to the house tomorrow before noon and see what happens."

"We could leave our snorkel equipment behind and then come back for it."

"Good idea," David said.

But the next day was a rainy one, and we didn't go to the lake. Mom and Dad were going into town. "Who wants to come with us?" Mom asked.

"I do," Lara said, jumping up.

I wasn't exactly happy about staying behind in that gloomy house in such miserable weather, but David spoke up for both of us, saying, "Meg and I will just stay here and play Monopoly."

As the car pulled out of the driveway, a crack of thunder made me jump, and I wished I had gone with them to town. It was only 11:30. We had thirty-five minutes to wait for the mysterious thing to happen again.

"Do you really want to play Monopoly?" I asked David.

"We may as well. It will help pass the time."

The minutes ticked by, each second marked by the swing of the pendulum. It was the longest half hour and five minutes of my life.

At noon we stopped playing, unable to concentrate on the game. Twelve long, dreary bongs sounded the hour. At precisely 12:05 we heard a noise like distant thunder, but with a deeper, longer rumbling. The floorboards shook beneath our feet; the dishes clinked in the cabinets; and as we watched in amazement, the little glass door to the clock swung open.

David and I looked at each other. Then we

began thumping each other on the back triumphantly. "The train!" we cried.

"It must go by every day at exactly 12:05!" I said.

"Of course! Why didn't we think of it before?" David said. "And the vibrations must be just enough to swing the door open and upset the pendulum."

"Now," I said, breathing freely once again, "how about that fifty dollars you owe me for landing on Boardwalk?"

The Mystery Prize

By Edith Gilmore

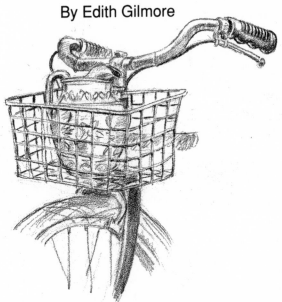

Our school fair was happening all over the big playground. I was happily watching a juggler when somebody grabbed my arm.

"Carlos! Emergency!" I jumped a foot and dropped my taffy apple. The grabber was my freckled friend Freddie, the most forgetful guy on Planet Earth. He was carrying a bowl of goldfish.

I glared at him. "What's the big idea?"

"Important case for you," gasped Freddie. "My bike! Stolen!"

"You forgot it somewhere."

"No, honest. It's missing from the bike rack here. But . . . er . . . I somehow left the lock at home. So I took a chance."

"You left your bike unlocked? Wow, are you in trouble."

"I know," moaned Freddie. "And I can't pay you to be my detective because I've already spent my money. But you're a pal of mine, Carlos, right?"

"Right," I agreed sadly.

"I'll give you my ticket for the mystery prize. I bought it in school yesterday. And I happened to see Mr. Hale wrapping up something that I think was a radio."

"It's a deal, Freddie." I knew that Mr. Hale, my homeroom teacher, was running the mystery-prize raffle. And I didn't have a radio. I used to have one, but my little brother got hold of a hammer and my radio at the same time.

I pulled my purple detective beanie out of my pocket. It seems to switch on my brain circuits. "Estimated time of robbery, client?" I inquired crisply as I headed for the bike rack.

"Let's see," muttered Freddie. "I was going to ride my bike here with my sister Elaine. But she kept hunting for her red sandals. And when she gave up, she got a phone call and began to gab. So I finally decided to ride here by myself. Ten blocks' biking time . . . I haven't been here even an hour, detective."

"Hmm. So if Elaine finally got here . . ."

"She's here. I saw her buying popcorn before I went to check on my bike."

"If she saw your bike still in the rack when she came, that will narrow the possible time of the crime. Find her and report to me at the scene of the theft."

Freddie saluted and rushed off.

I checked the rack. Two bikes. One was Elaine's old beat-up five-speed. Rear tire flat. The other I didn't recognize. Girl's bike: blue, new, initials *M. B.* on the fender.

Freddie came rushing back. "Found her! Come on."

Elaine was waiting in line at the art teacher's table. *(Cartoons drawn in full color—$1.00)* "My bike, Elaine!" yipped Freddie. "Swiped!"

"Very strange." Elaine ate some popcorn. "Because, of course, you locked it?"

"Elaine," I said mysteriously, "I observe you are wearing red sandals. Did you find them before you left home?"

"Listen, you half-pint Sherlock Holmes, I don't have to answer your questions."

"Yes you do," said Freddie, "if you want to

swap doing dinner dishes tonight the way you asked me to."

"Oh, well, okay. I forgot until I got here that Marie Barnes borrowed my red sandals. And Marie's home sick. So I went to her house and got them."

"Forgot!" said Freddie. "Ha, ha!"

I gave him a nudge. "Leave the witness to me, client. Now then, Elaine. You left home to come here after Freddie did. And since then you've been to Marie's house and back?"

"Sure."

"How? Your bike has a flat. And who owns the new blue bike in the rack with *M. B.* on it? Marie Barnes, maybe? But she's sick."

Elaine began to laugh. "Okay, okay. My bike got a flat on the way here. So I walked it. And when I saw Freddie's unlocked, I rode it home to give him a scare and so it wouldn't get stolen. I left it at home, got my sandals from Marie, and borrowed her bike."

"Off the hook!" yelped Freddie. "I forgive you, Elaine."

"You ought to thank me."

"Attention!" called Mr. Hale over the P.A. system. "Time for the mystery prize." I saw him shake a covered basket and look around. Dad was standing next to him with my little brother Mickey. Mr. Hale offered Mickey the basket.

"Pick a number, sonny." Mickey stuck his fat fist in and dug out a slip.

"Eighty-two," called Mr. Hale.

"I think that's it!" said Freddie. "You get the prize, Carlos."

"But where's the ticket?"

Freddie gulped. "I just remembered. Mom put a glass pitcher in my bike carrier for the antiques table. And I put the ticket in the pitcher. And I forgot the pitcher."

"No winner?" asked Mr. Hale. "Five minutes to claim the prize before we pick another number."

"Relax," said Elaine. "I gave the pitcher to the antiques table."

"Then it's probably sold!"

"Probably." Elaine fished in her pocket. "But I saw the ticket, and I took it out."

It was eighty-two. We rushed to Mr. Hale—just in time.

Freddie waited until I had unwrapped the radio and switched it on. Beautiful!

"Detective . . ." he began.

"What now?"

"I can't remember where I left my bowl of goldfish."

The Mystery of the Clanging Buoy

By Janet Poling

Anita woke up with a start. The howling wind that had rattled the house during the night was gone. But out on the channel, one of the bell buoys was noisily clanging.

"You hear that, too, Mitzy?" Anita asked the small brown terrier curled up at the foot of her bed. She got up and forced open the old wood-framed window. A slight breeze filled her small room with the salty smell of the ocean.

Clang-clang, clang-clang.

"There's hardly a ripple on the channel, but that buoy is rocking back and forth a mile a minute. Let's row out and take a closer look, huh, girl?" Anita scratched behind the dog's ears.

She quickly pulled on a T-shirt and jeans and hurried to the kitchen. Dad had to leave early this morning. Last night's storm must have made a mess on the docks, she thought.

Once she and Mitzy were outside, the bell buoy seemed to be ringing louder and faster than before. Anita ran and jumped over pieces of driftwood and piles of seaweed thrown onto the sand by the storm. Mitzy turned in circles along the shore and barked excitedly at the screeching sea gulls overhead.

"Boy, storms sure can cause a lick of trouble," Anita said, looking at a torn fishing net lying in a tangled heap on the sand.

Clang-clang, clang-clang.

Anita looked toward the noisy buoy across the channel. It was hard to tell, but she thought she saw something bobbing up and down in the water next to the buoy. "What is that out there?" she wondered.

The small rowboat sat in the wet sand near

the water. Anita untied the line that held the boat to an old wooden pier. From under the seat she took out a life jacket and fastened it over her T-shirt. Although Anita was a good swimmer, she always wore her life jacket in the boat.

"Come on, Mitzy. Let's go," Anita called, tugging the rowboat knee-deep into the cold water. Mitzy wagged her tail happily and took her place at the bottom of the boat as Anita climbed in.

Clang-clang, clang-clang.

The water was calm, and in no time at all the small rowboat was in the middle of the channel. Sunlight reflecting off the buoy made Anita squint. Then she saw something. It rose briefly out of the water and then sank under the waves, causing the bell on the buoy to clang rapidly.

"There *is* something over there," Anita said, rowing even harder now. Then she heard a funny sound. It was a shrill whistle coming from the direction of the buoy. "It's a dolphin!" Anita cried.

The dolphin's head rose out of the water and made the odd whistling noise again. Mitzy growled, then softly whimpered. "It's all right, Mitzy. Dolphins don't hurt people," Anita said, giving the terrier an affectionate pat. "Or dogs, either," she added.

When Anita reached the buoy, she could see

that the dolphin was tangled in a torn fishing net. "That dolphin is in trouble, Mitzy," Anita said with concern. "Dolphins need to breathe air, just as we do. That net that it's tangled in keeps pulling it under."

Anita tied on to the buoy. "Don't worry, dolphin. I'll help you," Anita whispered. She climbed carefully over the side of the boat into the cold, dark water. Mitzy gave a sharp yap as the dolphin nudged Anita gently with its wet nose.

The buoy clanged even louder. Anita pulled and tugged at the tangled netting, her life jacket keeping her afloat. "You're going to be just fine," Anita said, patting the dolphin. Working in the cold water was hard, but Anita finally managed to get the net off the dolphin's tail and fins. After that, it was able to wriggle free.

"Hurray!" Anita cried as the dolphin swam beyond the buoy, making joyful leaps and dives in and out of the water. Anita climbed quickly back into the rowboat. Mitzy greeted her happily, jumping into her lap and sticking her nose into Anita's face. "I'd better tell the Coast Guard about the net tangled on this buoy," Anita decided. "They can remove it to make sure this doesn't happen again."

The dolphin swam around and around the small boat as Anita began to row toward shore.

Then, in a final good-bye, it jumped high out of the water, made a graceful arc, and dove beneath the surface.

Smart Art
and the
Wheeler Dealers

By Sally Kellogg

In Pumpkin Center I'm known as Smart Art, Supersnooper and Troubleshooter. But I wasn't always Art, and I wasn't always considered so smart.

I was named Archibald Rodney Thanatopolis by my parents. That all changed when I learned to print my name. It didn't take me long to shorten it to A.R.T., just to save time and keep my fingers from cramping up. From then on I became just plain Art to almost everyone who knew me.

The "smart" part came the day after the big fire at Hanson's Hardware Store. Boy, what a fire! Fire engines wheeled down the street with their sirens shrieking. Everyone in town was there, even the Wheeler Dealers. They are a bunch of guys who have a secret club. I hadn't been asked to join, but I didn't really care much. My dog, Foghorn, and I were usually too busy, holed up in my bedroom laboratory working with my microscope and fingerprinting kit or fooling around with things to see what makes them work.

By the time Foghorn and I arrived at the scene, the fire fighters were squirting water onto the roof. With their oxygen masks they looked like creatures from another planet. But I was jolted back to earth by Mrs. Hanson, the store's owner, shrieking.

"There they are! Those are the boys, Officer McGreevey!" She pointed toward the Wheeler Dealers and, especially, right at Loose Tooth and Digger. "I had to chase them away from the back of the store as I was closing up. They were going through the empty cartons left from the French glassware I had just unpacked. And then, just before the fire trucks arrived," she continued, "I saw those same boys running out of the alley. Boys will usually run *to* a fire, not away from one."

Officer McGreevey scratched the top of his bald head. "Is that true, boys?" he asked. "Do you know anything about the fire?" He looked at Digger and Loose Tooth carefully.

"Sure, we were going through the trash," answered Digger, "looking for some boxes to store stuff in our clubhouse. Then we smelled smoke, and when we looked up, we saw flames in the front of the store. We ran as fast as we could to call the fire department."

"That's right, Officer," Loose Tooth echoed. He talks with a kind of whistle, as if he has a tooth that's ready to fall out.

"Well, boys, I'd like to ask you a few questions, since you were at the scene," Officer McGreevey went on.

Now Loose Tooth was really getting nervous. He whipped a handkerchief from his pocket to wipe his forehead, and out flew a book of matches, landing at Mrs. Hanson's feet. "Aha! I told you so," she sputtered indignantly. "There's the evidence right in front of your eyes, Officer."

Poor Loose Tooth. He had never been suspected of a crime before. He was shaking like a canary in a snowstorm. I didn't think he'd be able to talk, but somehow he managed. "We found those matches in the alley," he whimpered, "and were taking them home so no little kids could get them. We didn't start any fire."

Officer McGreevey rubbed his chin thoughtfully.

I decided to step in. "Officer McGreevey, I'd like to check the fingerprints on those matches," I said.

"Well, all right, Art," he answered. "I think I have all the evidence I need."

After dinner I carefully sprinkled talcum powder on the matchbook cover. Then I lifted the prints off with transparent tape and taped them to one of my file cards. As I was sitting there thinking, I flipped open the matchbook. All the matches were there. And the striker had never been scratched at all. The matches had never been used!

The next day I returned to the hardware store, where I found Mrs. Hanson busy sweeping up broken glass. Boy, was it a mess! "You certainly have a lot of damage, Mrs. Hanson," I said. "Too bad so much of your glassware was broken. But I see you still have some left."

I had to squint as the bright sunlight bounced off the remaining French glassware. Mrs. Hanson had wiped the soot from the unbroken glasses and set them back on the shelf. Mrs. Hanson moaned. "Yes, a few glasses are left," she answered. "But I can't say the same for the wrapping paper on the shelf just behind."

I looked at the blackened display case behind the glassware. Suddenly, I had an idea. Taking a page out of my notebook, I carefully put it in a sunny spot on the burned-out rack behind the glassware display. I stuck around, helping Mrs. Hanson clean up the mess while I kept my eye on the paper. Soon, just as I suspected, small wisps of smoke curled upward from the paper.

"Look, Mrs. Hanson!" I cried. "The sun started the fire. Its rays were concentrated by the glassware, and they ignited your wrapping paper."

Well, to make a long story short, the news of my discovery spread faster than the fire at Hanson's Hardware Store. The Wheeler Dealers asked me to join their club, where I act as special consultant on important problems. And as a new member I was given my own special name—Smart Art.

The Case
of the
Missing Science Book

By Jeanne Iacono Martin

Bonnie Shults came storming into Tracy Fletcher's Detective Agency. Tracy looked up from her desk. "You look as mad as a bear with a bee sting," she said.

"I've been stung," said Bonnie, "and for ten dollars. That's how much it's going to cost to buy a new science book for school. Mine's been stolen!"

"I'll take your case," said Tracy. She opened her notebook and wrote *Case of the Missing Science Book.*

"Where did you last see the book?"

"On our patio table."

"Do you have any idea who took it?"

"I don't like to accuse anyone." Bonnie hesitated.

"Of course not," said Tracy, "but all detectives need to have suspects."

"Maybe Kevin."

"Your next-door neighbor? He's one of the most honest people at school."

"I know," said Bonnie. "But he's the only

person I've seen outside today. Just Kevin and his robot."

"His robot!"

"It's his parents', but Kevin says he's also responsible for it sometimes."

"Let's go see him," said Tracy.

The two girls hurried to Kevin's house. Kevin answered the door. "Hi. What's up?"

"Bonnie says you have a robot. May I see it?"

"Sure." Kevin led the girls into the kitchen. "There." He pointed to a gleaming barrel-shaped object riding on wheels. Its metallic arms were moving smoothly, cleaning the stove.

"How does it do that?" asked Bonnie.

"You program it by pushing buttons on the middle of its chest."

"Can you program it?" asked Tracy.

"Sure. A mechanic came from the robot factory and taught the entire family."

"What else did it do today?" asked Tracy.

"Well, this morning I took it outside so it could clean the backyard and cut the grass. It's great not having to mow the lawn anymore on Saturdays."

"Let's go see a robot-mowed lawn," said Tracy. Both girls giggled. As soon as they entered the backyard, Tracy said in a surprised tone, "Why, this grass hasn't been cut today!"

"It sure hasn't," said Kevin. "Maybe the robot can't use a power mower."

Tracy wrote in her notebook *Clue #1—Robot did not cut grass.* Tracy turned to Kevin. "Were you outside this morning, too?" she asked.

"Only when I took the robot outside to program it. The rest of the time I was inside reading about model rockets."

"Don't you have to watch and see that the robot doesn't make mistakes?" asked Bonnie.

"No," said Kevin. "Robots don't make mistakes. They do exactly what they are told to. Now let's go inside. The robot has probably finished cleaning the kitchen. I'll show you how

I program it to clean the study."

The robot was standing quietly in a corner of the laundry room. "This is its station," explained Kevin. "It comes here when it is done and automatically shuts off."

Tracy looked into the kitchen. "This floor is immaculate. Your robot is a good housekeeper but a bad yard keeper!"

"I guess so," said Kevin. "Now I'll show you how to program the robot to clean the study. It will dust and put all the books back on the shelves. All I do is punch three numbers: 514. No. Wait. I mean 415. Okay, watch."

"Stop," said Tracy. She wrote *Clue #2— Humans can make mistakes*. "Kevin, will 514 program the robot?"

"Yes, every three-digit number tells it to do something; 514 programs the robot to clean the backyard and cut the grass."

"I see," said Tracy. She faced Bonnie. "I have an idea where your science book is."

"You do?" Bonnie was astonished by her statement.

"The clues lead to it," said Tracy. She explained. "Robots might not make mistakes, but humans do. Kevin pushed 415 instead of 514, programming the robot to clean the study instead of mowing the backyard. The robot began to search for a place that resembled a study. It went to the nearest door, the gate separating your yards. Upon finding Bonnie's patio full of furniture, the robot began to react as if in the study. It took the science book from the patio table and . . ."

"It did?" Bonnie was amazed.

"But then," continued Tracy, "the robot had to find shelves."

"I know," said Kevin. "When I opened the back door so it could return to its station, it went first to the study and put Bonnie's book in the bookcase."

"No. The robot had already straightened what it mistakenly believed was the study," said Tracy, "so I think Bonnie's book is still somewhere in her backyard."

They ran to Bonnie's backyard. Kevin and Bonnie began looking. Tracy just stood there and thought.

"It's not here," hollered Kevin.

"Yes, it is," said Tracy. "Just look for something that would resemble a bookshelf to a robot."

"We've looked behind flower boxes and near the tool shelf," said Bonnie.

Tracy sat down to think again. After a few long silent minutes, she jumped to her feet. "The slats of the picket fence," she said.

The three dashed to the fence and began

searching. Suddenly Kevin yelled, "Here it is!"

"It sure is," Bonnie said. She turned to Tracy. "You are an amazing detective."

"The best," added Kevin.

Tracy smiled. She wrote in her notebook *Case of the Missing Science Book—solved*.

Mystery of the Missing Mouse

By Tina Tibbitts

Even if my Aunt Phyllis didn't pay me, I'd still help out in her pet shop Saturdays, because that's when I get to spend the most time with my mouse, Bartholomew. The work isn't too exciting—cleaning cages and aquariums—but the shop is just like my own private zoo. You see, because of my sister's allergies, I can't have any animals at home. And I do have my own special apron with my name on it, just like a real salesperson.

One warm Saturday morning when I got to the pet shop, the door was propped open. "Hi, Aunt Phyllis," I called as I entered.

"Good morning, Tricia!" Out of the storeroom came Aunt Phyllis, pushing a cart loaded with kitty-litter bags. From his cage across the room Bartholomew squeaked his usual greeting.

"Well, hello yourself," I said, tying on my bib apron as I walked over. I took him out of the cage and dropped him into my apron pocket. "There's a caramel in there," I whispered, "so enjoy yourself while I clean up your messy house."

I was just finishing when a customer came into the shop. As Aunt Phyllis went over to help him, she asked me to finish sweeping up kitty litter that had spilled across the floor. It took a while to clean up, and I forgot Bartholomew until Aunt Phyllis noticed his empty cage.

"He's right here," I said, patting my apron pocket. But it felt empty. When I looked inside, all I saw was a hole where the caramel had been.

We searched everywhere but couldn't find Bartholomew. "He must have gone out the open door," said Aunt Phyllis.

"But he wouldn't run away," I wailed. "He's my friend."

Aunt Phyllis spoke gently. "Tricia, he's a mouse. You must expect him to behave like one."

I was afraid I'd start blubbering, so I ran to the door. The only thing on the sidewalk was a puddle of ice cream. It was strawberry, Bartholomew's favorite kind. But wait—why wasn't he eating it? Had something scared him away? Or had he startled the owner of the ice cream into spilling it?

Melted ice cream trailing away from the puddle showed the direction the ice-cream eater had been going. I followed it, looking right and left for a place where a fleeing mouse could hide. I stopped outside Andrade's Shoe Store. Racks of shoes for sale stood on the sidewalk.

"Mrs. Andrade, have you seen a mouse come this way?" I asked.

She laughed. "I suppose you mean the one being chased by the dog and the girl smeared with ice cream. That little mouse scrambled into some of my best shoes, and the dog dived in after it. My display would have been ruined if the boy on the bicycle hadn't stopped and picked up the mouse."

"Then what did he do?"

"Buttoned the mouse inside his jacket pocket. I heard the girl say she thought it came from the pet shop."

"Where did the boy go?"

"Up toward the post office. He had a package to mail."

I thanked Mrs. Andrade and ran to the post office. But inside there was no sign of the package kid, so I asked Mrs. Sweeney about him. "Yes, a boy mailed a package here a while ago," she said, "but I don't know his name. I do remember the package was going to a Mr. Nelson in California, and the mail truck just left."

My heart sank. After all that, I wasn't any closer to finding Bartholomew. I trudged glumly back to the pet shop. My only chance was that maybe Mr. Nelson was a relative and the package kid had the same last name. It was a long shot, but I had no better clue.

Aunt Phyllis heard my story with a sympathetic smile and wished me luck as I began calling the nine Nelsons in the phone book. I felt stupid asking each person if a boy who'd mailed a package in the morning lived there. I got two *no*'s, a busy signal, and a lady who yelled something about telephone salespeople and hung up. Just then a boy came into the pet shop. He wore a jacket with buttoned pockets, and one of them bulged.

"Excuse me," he inquired, "is one of your mice missing?"

"So you're the mouse-napper!" I cried. "I tracked you to the post office, and I've been calling all the Nelsons in town."

He looked embarrassed. "Sorry I didn't return it sooner. You see, my little brother would like a pet mouse, but all Mom and Dad say is 'Absolutely not.'"

"I know what that feels like," I admitted, calming down.

"I stopped at home so my brother could play with the mouse a little before I came back to see if it was from here." He handed Bartholomew over to me.

I was so happy to have my little friend back I felt generous. "Bartholomew belongs to me," I explained. "But if your parents don't mind, I'll bring him over to play sometime."

"That'd be great! By the way, I'm Gary Nelson, and you're one smart detective, Tricia."

"I didn't tell you my name."

Gary grinned. "You didn't have to." He pointed to my apron.

"You'd make a good detective, too," I said.

We laughed together.

The Hayride Mystery

By Rosalie Maggio

"Get off my leg!"

"Ouch, you stepped on my hand."

"Catch him, somebody, before he falls off!"

It didn't take a detective to know that Hawkeye was making his way from the back of the straw-filled hayrack to where I was sitting in the front. And, anyway, Hawkeye is the one who thinks he's a detective, not me. His name isn't really Hawkeye, but he says he never heard of a detective named Bill so we have to call him Hawkeye.

Our whole gang had turned out for Morton's hayride, and I think Hawkeye managed to step on every one of them before he tripped over my feet and landed next to me. Absent-mindedly, he tried to brush away Morton's dog, Peabody, who was chewing on Hawkeye's pant leg.

"Every year," he said, "I tell myself I'm never going on another one of Morton's hayrides. I'm allergic to hay. It's always freezing cold. Morton's dog hates me." He stopped long enough to remove Peabody's teeth from his sweater. "We're being pulled along by a pair of killer horses. And I can't sleep for months afterward because of the ghost stories."

Right on cue, somebody passed us a couple of popcorn balls, and Ellie started telling the first ghost story. Hawkeye hummed softly. I knew he was trying not to listen. He didn't even notice that Peabody was eating his popcorn ball. Ellie's story was mostly low moaning noises, and everybody screamed a lot. About halfway through, Hawkeye hissed, "Look in the woods! See those little red eyes? Those are wild animals!"

I pried his hand off my arm and said, "That's ridiculous."

"No, it's not," he said. "These woods are full of pumas and wild boars."

"Hawkeye," I said, "what you are seeing is a reflection from spiders' eyes. It's a scientific phenomenon called eyeshine."

Hawkeye drew himself up and snapped, "I knew that!"

After Ellie's story, Charlie had one. He was just getting going pretty good when Morton let out an awful yell. I turned around to tell him the story wasn't *that* scary. But Morton wasn't anywhere on the hay wagon. Everybody else was looking for him, too.

"Hawkeye," I said, "here's your chance to show us what a great detective you are. Where's Morton?"

"A ghost has gotten him!" shouted Hawkeye. "Or one of those wild animals! I knew it!"

"There's probably a reasonable explanation for this," I said.

"Reasonable?" said Hawkeye. "You call it reasonable to be carried off by wild animals?"

"Look," I said, "there's Morton behind us on the road. He fell off!"

"I knew that!" said Hawkeye.

But as it turned out, Morton hadn't just fallen. He said he had been pushed!

As we bumped and jolted our way back to the farmhouse, we tried to figure out what had happened. But nobody admitted pushing him, and Morton wouldn't change his story.

We were all quiet as we sat around in Morton's kitchen drinking hot apple cider and dunking doughnuts. Finally Hawkeye said, "I think this is a case for a detective." We all knew who he was talking about. But before he could get started, I felt I should point out something. "Hawkeye," I said, "your cup has a hole in it."

"You can't fool me," he said. "There's nothing wrong with my cup."

I watched the cider dripping onto his leg and said, "Hawkeye, it has a hole in it."

Hawkeye looked at the cider running off his elbow and said, "I knew that!"

After getting another cup, he began pacing

back and forth. "You, Margaret!" he said. "You were mad at Morton for getting the highest grade in the math test. So you pushed him." Before Margaret could do more than gasp, he was pointing at Tony. "I saw you and Morton arguing last week," he said. Within minutes Hawkeye had accused every one of us of pushing Morton off the hayrack.

It was time for a little help from a friend. I said, "So what you're telling us, Hawkeye, is that somebody in this room pushed Morton."

Hawkeye swung around and said, "No, I'm not!"

"I get the idea," I insisted, winking broadly, "that you think it was one of us."

"I knew that!" he said.

"But," I continued, "what nobody except you seems to realize is that we weren't the only ones on the hay wagon!"

"We weren't?" he gasped. "Oh, no! Ghosts! It was a ghost!"

I sighed. "As you were saying, Hawkeye, if it wasn't ghosts, and it wasn't one of us, it must have been . . ." I paused. For a moment, nobody breathed. Nobody but Peabody, of course, who was pushing a doughnut around on the floor with one large paw.

It was an idea whose time had come. The light dawned. Everybody seemed to see it at once. "Peabody!" they yelled. "It was Peabody!"

Hawkeye's eyes widened. He said, "I believe that's the most ridiculous . . ."

Morton interrupted excitedly, "That's it! Those weren't hands on my back. They were paws! I remember the feeling. Peabody did it!"

And that's when I learned the secret of being a great detective. Hawkeye looked us all straight in the eye and said confidently, "I knew that!"